Mr. Strong is so strong he can throw a cannonball as far as you or I can throw a tennis ball!

Mr. Strong is so strong he can hammer nails into a wall just by tapping them with his finger.

Strong by name and strong by nature!

And would you like to know the secret of Mr. Strong's strength?

Eggs!

The more eggs Mr. Strong eats, the stronger he becomes.

Stronger, and stronger, and stronger!

Anyway, this is about a funny thing that happened to Mr. Strong one day.

That morning he was having breakfast.

And for breakfast he was having...eggs!

Followed by eggs. And to finish, he was having—guess what?

That's right. Eggs!

That was Mr. Strong's normal breakfast.

After his eggy breakfast, Mr. Strong brushed his teeth.

And, as usual, he squeezed all the toothpaste out of the tube.

And, as usual, he brushed his teeth so hard he broke his toothbrush.

Mr. Strong goes through a lot of toothpaste and toothbrushes!

After that he decided to take a walk.

He put on his hat and opened the front door of his house. Crash!

"What a beautiful day," he thought to himself, and stepping outside his house, he shut his front door.

Bang! The door fell off its hinges.

Mr. Strong goes through a lot of front doors!

Then Mr. Strong went for his walk.

He walked through the woods.

But he wasn't looking where he was going and walked slam-bang into a huge tree. Crack!

The huge tree trunk snapped, and the tree thundered to the ground.

"Whoops!" said Mr. Strong.

He walked into town.

And again, not looking where he was going, he walked slam-bang straight into a bus!

Now, as you know, if you or I were to walk into a bus, we'd get run over.

Wouldn't we?

Not Mr. Strong!

The bus stopped as if it had run into a brick wall.

"Whoops!" said Mr. Strong.

Eventually, Mr. Strong walked through the town and out into the country.

He met a very worried-looking farmer on the road.

"What's the matter?" asked Mr. Strong.

"It's my cornfield," replied the farmer. "It's on fire and I can't put it out!"

Mr. Strong looked over the hedge, and, sure enough, the cornfield was blazing fiercely.

"Water!" said Mr. Strong. "We must get water to put out the fire!"

"But I don't have enough water to put a whole field out," cried the worried farmer, "and the nearest water is down at the river, and I don't have a pump!"

"Then we'll have to find something to carry the water in," replied Mr. Strong.

"Is that your barn?" he asked the farmer, pointing to a barn in another field.

"Yes, I was going to put my corn in it," said the farmer. "But..."

"Can I use it?" asked Mr. Strong.

"Yes, but..." replied the perplexed farmer.

Mr. Strong walked over to the barn, and then do you know what he did?

He picked it up. He actually picked up the barn!

The farmer couldn't believe his eyes.

Then Mr. Strong carried the barn, over his head, down to the river.

Then he turned the barn upside down.

Then he lowered it into the river so that it filled up with water.

Then, and this really shows how strong Mr. Strong is, he picked it up and carried it back to the blazing cornfield.

Mr. Strong emptied the upside-down barn full of water over the flames.

Sizzle. Sizzle. Splutter. Splutter.

One minute the flames were leaping into the air. The next minute they were gone.

"How can I ever thank you?" the farmer asked Mr. Strong.

"Oh, it was nothing," remarked Mr. Strong modestly.

"But I must find some way to reward you," said the farmer.

"Well," said Mr. Strong, "you're a farmer, so you must have some chickens."

"Yes, lots," said the farmer.

"And chickens lay eggs," went on Mr. Strong, "and I love eggs!"

"Then you shall have as many eggs as you can carry," said the farmer, and took Mr. Strong over to the farmyard.

Mr. Strong said good-bye to the farmer and thanked him for the eggs, and the farmer thanked Mr. Strong for helping.

Then Mr. Strong, using just one finger, picked up the eggs and went home.

Mr. Strong put the eggs down carefully on his kitchen table and went to close the kitchen door.

Crash! The door fell off its hinges.

"Whoops!" said Mr. Strong, and started cooking his lunch. And for lunch he was starting with eggs. Followed by an egg or two. And then eggs. And then for his dessert he was having...

Well, can you guess? If you can, there's no need to turn this page to find out he was having...

Ice cream!
Ha! Ha!